GOOD KING WENCESLAS

JOHN M. NEALE ❧ TIM LADWIG

Eerdmans Books for Young Readers

Grand Rapids, Michigan • Cambridge, U.K.

In memory of George Bauer, who loved
the Czech people and the city of Prague
— *T.L.*

Copyright © 2005 Tim Ladwig
Published in 2005 by Eerdmans Books for Young Readers
An imprint of Wm. B. Eerdmans Publishing Company
255 Jefferson S.E., Grand Rapids, Michigan 49503
P.O. Box 163, Cambridge CB3 9PU U.K.

05 06 07 08 09 10   8 7 6 5 4 3 2 1

Library of Congress Cataloging-in-Publication Data

Neale, J. M. (John Mason), 1818-1866.
Good King Wenceslas / original song written by John M. Neale ; illustrated by Tim Ladwig.
p. cm.
Summary: Illustrated text of the carol about the kindness of Wenceslas, duke of Bohemia.

ISBN 0-8028-5209-2 (alk. paper)

1. Carols, English--Texts. 2. Wenceslas, Duke of Bohemia, ca. 907-929--Juvenile literature.
3. Christmas music--Texts. [1. Carols. 2. Christmas music. 3. Wenceslas, Duke of Bohemia, ca. 907-929.]
I. Ladwig, Tim, ill. II. Title.
PZ8.3.G5885 2005
782.28'1723--dc22
[[
2004010237

The display type was hand-lettered by John Stevens.
The text type is set in Plantin.
The illustrations were created with watercolor, liquid acrylic, and oil on paper.
Gayle Brown, Art Director
Matthew Van Zomeren, Graphic Designer

In the city of Prague, in the Czech Republic, there is a square,
and in the square is a statue of the country's patron saint.

At Christmastime tales are still told
and songs still sung about him.

And children still imagine
a long time ago . . .

Good King Wenceslas looked out
on the Feast of Stephen,
when the snow lay round about,
deep and crisp and even.

Brightly shone the moon that night,
though the frost was cruel,
when a poor man came in sight,
gathering winter fuel.

"Hither, page, and stand by me,
   if thou knowest it, telling,
yonder peasant, who is he?
   Where and what his dwelling?"

"Sire, he lives a good league hence,
   underneath the mountain,
right against the forest fence,
   by Saint Agnes' fountain."

"Bring me food and bring me wine.
Bring me pine logs hither.
Thou and I will see him dine
when we bear them thither."

Page and monarch forth they went,
forth they went together,

through the rude wind's wild lament
and the bitter weather.

"Sire, the night is darker now
and the wind blows stronger.
Fails my heart, I know not how,
I can go no longer."

"Mark my footsteps, my good page;
tread thou in them boldly.
Thou shalt find the winter's rage
freeze thy blood less coldly."

In his master's steps he trod,
where the snow lay dinted.

Heat was in the very sod
which the saint had printed.

Therefore, Christians all, be sure,
wealth or rank possessing,
ye who now will bless the poor,
shall yourselves find blessing.

Historical Note

The beloved Christmas carol "Good King Wenceslas" tells the story of a real tenth-century king who was well known for his generosity and Christian spirit.

Vaclav Wenceslas was born in Bohemia, which is now part of the Czech Republic. Born into the royal family, Wenceslas was raised by his grandmother to be a devout Christian. His father died when he was only thirteen years old, and five years later Wenceslas became king. Young King Wenceslas ruled the land fairly, gave aid to the poor, and sought to spread Christianity throughout Bohemia.

In 1853 John Mason Neale, an Anglican priest who lived in England, heard stories of the Bohemian king's kindness and wrote "Good King Wenceslas" to inspire children to be generous on Saint Stephen's Day (December 26). The music for the song comes from a spring carol that was first published in 1582.

The Christmas song portrays Wenceslas the way the people of his time knew him — a compassionate man who was especially kind to children, orphans, and slaves.

The original words of the song have been adapted slightly in this book for today's young readers. John Mason Neale's original words appear with the music on the final page.

Good King Wenceslas

John M. Neale, 1853   Traditional

1. Good King Wen-ces-las look'd out on the feast of Ste-phen,
2. "Hith-er, page, and stand by me, if thou know'st it, tell-ing,
3. "Bring me flesh and bring me wine, bring me pine logs hith-er.
4. "Sire, the night is dark-er now, and the wind blows strong-er.
5. In his mas-ter's steps he trod, where the snow lay dint-ed.

When the snow lay round a-bout, deep and crisp and e-ven.
Yon-der peas-ant, who is he? Where and what his dwell-ing?"
Thou and I will see him dine, when we bear them thith-er."
Fails my heart, I know not how, I can go no long-er."
Heat was in the ver-y sod which the saint had print-ed.

Bright-ly shone the moon that night, though the frost was cru-el,
"Sire, he lives a good league hence, un-der-neath the moun-tain;
Page and mon-arch forth they went, forth they went to-geth-er,
"Mark my foot-steps, my good page, tread thou in them bold-ly.
There-fore, Chris-tian men, be sure, wealth or rank pos-sess-ing;

When a poor man came in sight, gath-'ring win-ter fu-el.
Right a-gainst the for-est fence by Saint Ag-nes' foun-tain."
Through the rude wind's wild la-ment and the bit-ter weath-er.
Thou shalt find the win-ter's rage freeze thy blood less cold-ly."
Ye who now will bless the poor shall your-selves find bless-ing;